Said a Flea to his dog . . .

"It's not you—
it is me!
Can't you see that this
flea simply *needs* to be
FREE?

"Free to see other dogs.

Free to
hop.

Free to
r o a m.

I'm hoping to find
A **new dog** for my home!

Too **tall.**

Too **short.**

"Too hairy.

Too scary.

Too chasing-a-ball.

Too quiet

and sneaky.

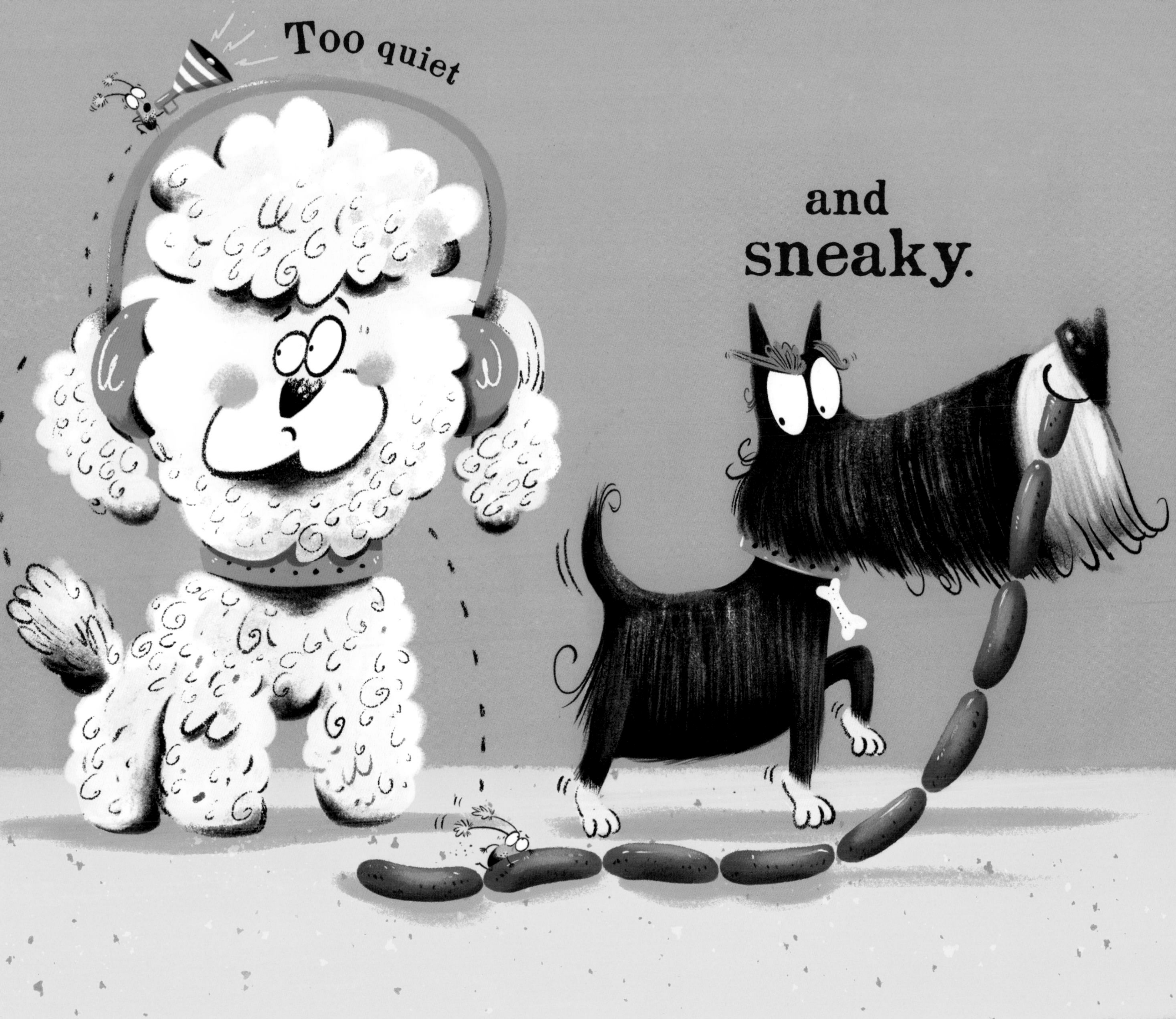

"Too **dirty**.

Too **clean**.

Too greedy.

Too lean.

"Too **busy**.

Too **calm**.

Too **city**.

Too **farm**.

But who's
in the kennel ...?

"It's *hard* to find perfect.
I've searched day and night.

"A wonderful sight!

A skip and a jump. A leap

and a bound.

It's the dog I'd forgotten . . .

For Gaia, Aster and little Jonty – W.M.

For Thomas X – N.R.

HODDER CHILDREN'S BOOKS
First published in Great Britain in 2021
by Hodder and Stoughton

Text copyright ©
Will Mabbitt, 2021
Illustration copyright ©
Nathan Reed, 2021

A CIP catalogue record
for this book is available
from the British Library.

HB ISBN: 978 1 444 95077 9
PB ISBN: 978 1 444 95078 6

10 9 8 7 6 5 4 3 2 1

Printed and bound in China

Hodder Children's Books,
an imprint of Hachette
Children's Group,
part of Hodder and Stoughton
Carmelite House,
50 Victoria Embankment,
London, EC4Y 0DZ
An Hachette UK Company
www.hachette.co.uk
www.hachettechildrens.co.uk

FSC® C104740
MIX
Paper from
responsible sources
FSC
www.fsc.org

h
Hodder
Children's
Books